The POKY LITTLE PUPPY

and
Other Stories to Color

A GOLDEN BOOK • NEW YORK

Copyright © 2007 by Random House, Inc. All rights reserved. Published in the United States by Golden Books, an imprint of Random House Children's Books, a division of Random House, Inc., New York. The stories contained in this work were originally published in slightly different form as follows: *The Poky Little Puppy,* written by Janette Sebring Lowrey, illustrated by Gustaf Tenggren, copyright © 1942, renewed 1976 by Random House, Inc., originally published by Simon & Schuster, Inc., and Artists and Writers Guild, Inc., in 1942; *The Shy Little Kitten,* written by Cathleen Schurr, illustrated by Gustaf Tenggren, copyright © 1946, renewed 1977 by Random House, Inc., originally published by Simon & Schuster, Inc., and Artists and Writers Guild, Inc., in 1946; and *The Fuzzy Duckling,* written by Jane Werner Watson, illustrated by Alice and Martin Provensen, copyright © 1948, renewed 1977 by Random House, Inc. The illustrations in this work are adapted from the original illustrations. A Golden Book, A Little Golden Book, the G colophon, and the distinctive gold spine are registered trademarks of Random House, Inc. A Little Golden Book Classic is a trademark of Random House, Inc. The Poky Little Puppy is a registered trademark and The Shy Little Kitten and The Fuzzy Duckling are trademarks of Random House, Inc.

ISBN: 978-0-375-83536-0

www.goldenbooks.com

www.randomhouse.com/kids

Printed in the United States of America

10 9 8 7 6 5 4

The POKY LITTLE PUPPY

The poky little puppy and his four brothers and sisters were full of mischief.

One day, the five little puppies dug a hole under the
fence. Poky was the last one through.

They went for a walk in the wide, wide world.

Through the meadow they went, down the
road, over the bridge . . .

. . . across the green grass, and up a hill, one
right after the other.

When they got to the top of the hill, one little puppy wasn't there. "Now, where in the world is that poky little puppy?" they wondered.

He certainly wasn't at the top of the hill.
Connect the dots to see what is there.

The poky little puppy wasn't going down the other side of the hill. The only thing going down was a fuzzy caterpillar.

Help the fuzzy caterpillar get down the hill to the patch of bluebells.

START

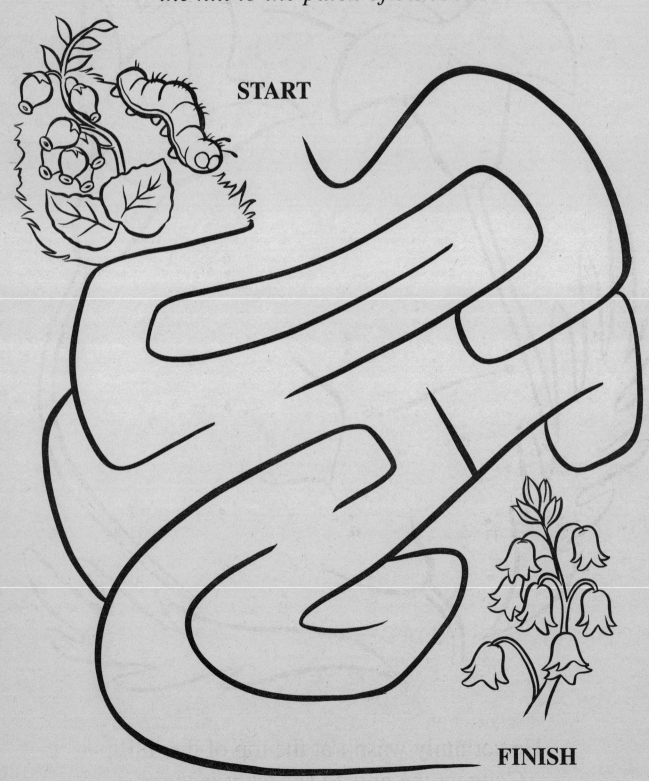

FINISH

The poky little puppy wasn't coming up this side. The only thing the other puppies could see coming up was a quick green lizard.

When the four puppies looked down at
the bottom of the hill . . .

. . . there was the poky little puppy running round
and round, his nose to the ground.

Help the four puppies get to Poky.

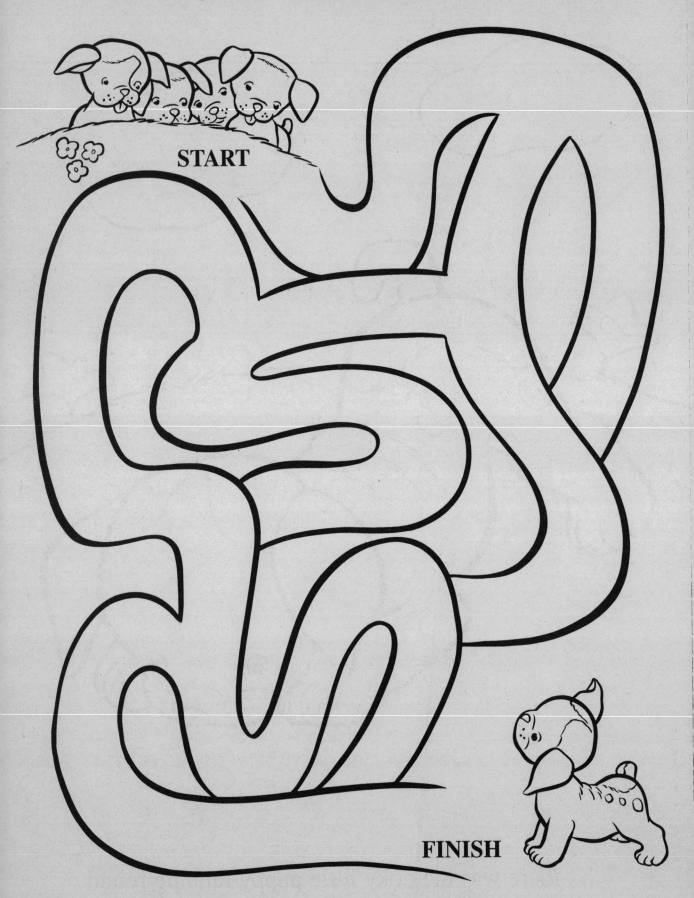

START

FINISH

And down they went to see, roly-poly, pell-mell,
tumble-bumble, till they came to the green grass;
and there they stopped short.

"I smell something!" said the poky little puppy. Then the four little puppies began to sniff, and they smelled it, too.

The puppies smell the rice pudding that is waiting for them at home!

Connect the dots.

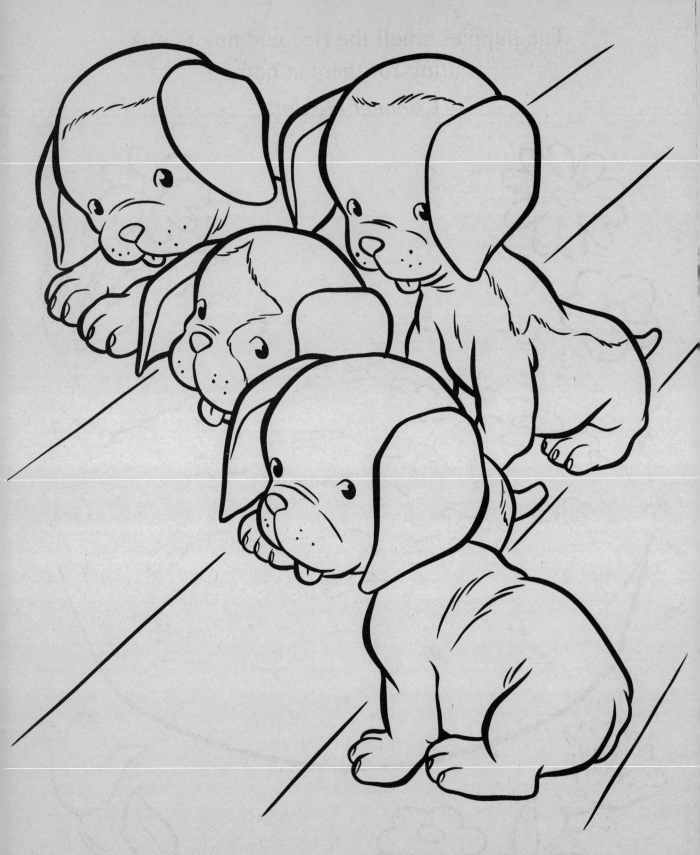

The four puppies rushed home, but they didn't get any pudding because their mother was angry. She did not like them digging holes under fences. She made them go right to bed.

But the poky little puppy came home after everyone was sound asleep.

He ate up all the rice pudding and crawled into bed as happy as a lark.

The next morning, someone had filled the hole and put up a sign. But the five little puppies dug a hole under the fence anyway and went for a walk in the wide, wide world.

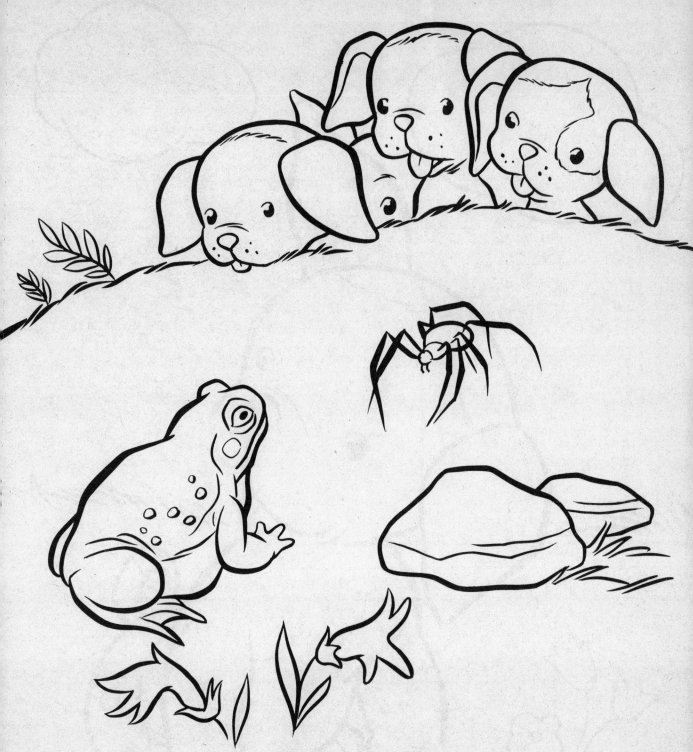

Up the hill they went! Once more, the four puppies
couldn't see the poky little puppy. He wasn't going
down the other side of the hill. The only thing there
was a big black spider. And the only thing coming
up was a brown hop-toad.

The poky little puppy was at the bottom of the hill.
He could hear his mother spooning chocolate custard
into the puppies' bowls at home!

The four little puppies could hear it, too. And they rushed home to get some custard.

But the four puppies didn't get any custard because
they had dug a hole under the fence. They had to go
straight to bed.

But the poky little puppy came home after everyone else
was sound asleep, and he ate up all the chocolate custard!

The next day, the five puppies dug a hole under the fence and went up the hill. And again, the others couldn't find the poky little puppy! He wasn't going down the other side. The only thing going down was a little grass snake.

He wasn't coming up this side of the hill. The only thing coming up was a big grasshopper.

The puppies see the poky little puppy at the
bottom of the hill.

Help them get down to him!

START

FINISH

A ripe, red strawberry! The puppies suddenly
remembered: strawberry shortcake was waiting for them
at home! The four puppies rushed home, but the poky
little puppy stayed to look at the strawberry.

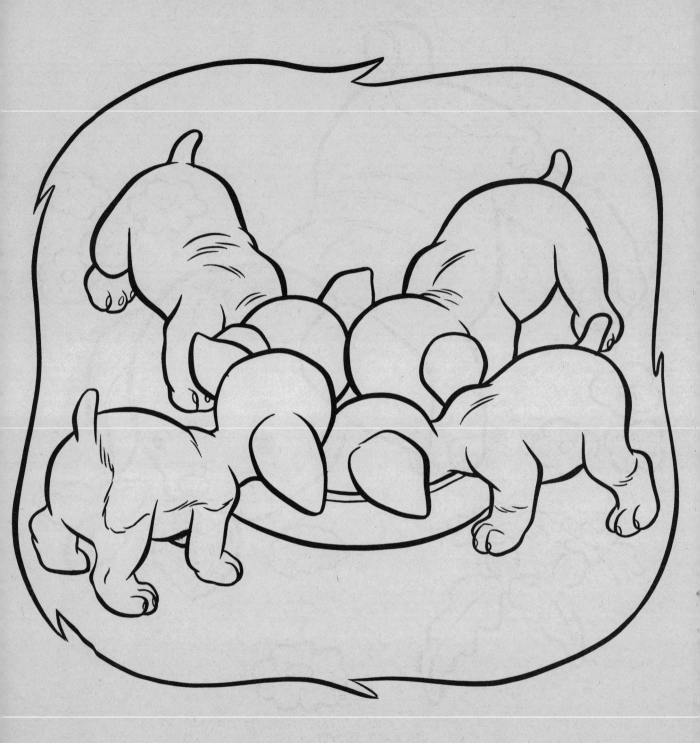

This time, the four puppies decided to fill up the hole after they got home. Their mother was so happy that she let them eat the strawberry shortcake.

And this time, when the poky little puppy got home, he had to squeeze through the fence. By the time he got there, all the shortcake had been eaten. "Dear me!" said his mother. "What a pity you're so poky! Now the strawberry shortcake is all gone!"

And the next morning, someone had put up a sign. The poky little puppy would never be poky again, and he would always get dessert!

THE SHY LITTLE KITTEN

Way up in the hayloft of an old red barn lived a mother cat and her new baby kittens. There were five bold and frisky little roly-poly kittens . . .

. . . and one little striped kitten who was very, very shy.

All the animals on the farm came to bring presents for
the new baby kittens. The rabbit came with carrots
and crisp green lettuce.

The pig brought apples.

The goose carried strawberries wrapped in catnip leaves.

Even the big hen, looking very, very wise, came and laid a white egg in the hay for the new babies.

Look at the last page. What is different in this picture?
Circle everything you find.

What present would you bring to the kittens?
Draw it.

The mother cat told her kittens that they would all go and thank the farm animals for their presents. So the five little roly-poly kittens . . .

. . . and the one little roly-poly striped kitten who was very, very shy all sat down and washed their faces and paws with busy little red tongues.

Then off the kittens marched, straight out of the cool, dark barn, into the warm sunshine. The five bold and frisky little kittens kicked up their heels with joy!

But the shy little kitten just stood off by herself at the end of the line.

That was how the shy little kitten happened to see the earth push up in a little mound right in front of her. Then—*pop!*—up came a pointed little nose. The nose belonged to a chubby mole.

"Good morning!" said the mole. "Won't you come for a walk with me?" The shy little kitten was about to say no, but the mother cat and her five frisky kittens had disappeared from sight.

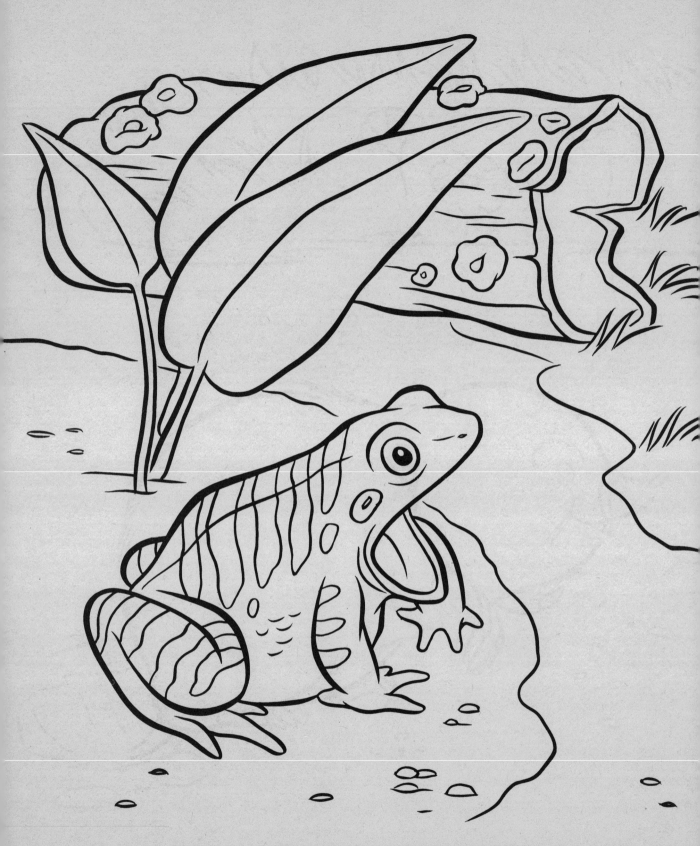

So the shy little kitten went walking with the chubby
mole. Soon they met a speckled frog. "My, what big
eyes he has!" whispered the shy little kitten.
But the frog had sharp ears, too.

"My mouth is much bigger. Look!" And the frog opened his great cave of a mouth. The mole and the kitten laughed and laughed until their sides ached.

"I really should be getting back to my mother and the others," said the shy little kitten, "but I don't know where to find them."

"I'll show you," said a strange voice. And out of the
bushes bounded a shaggy black puppy.

But the shaggy puppy stopped to bark, "Woof, woof," at a red squirrel in a tree. He was full of mischief.

"Chee, chee, chee," the squirrel chattered back. And she dropped a hickory nut right on the puppy's nose. She was very brave.

Soon the kitten and the puppy came bounding out of the
woods, and there before them stretched the farmyard.

"Here we are," said the shaggy puppy dog. And down the
hillside they raced, across the bridge, above the brook,
and straight on into the farmyard.

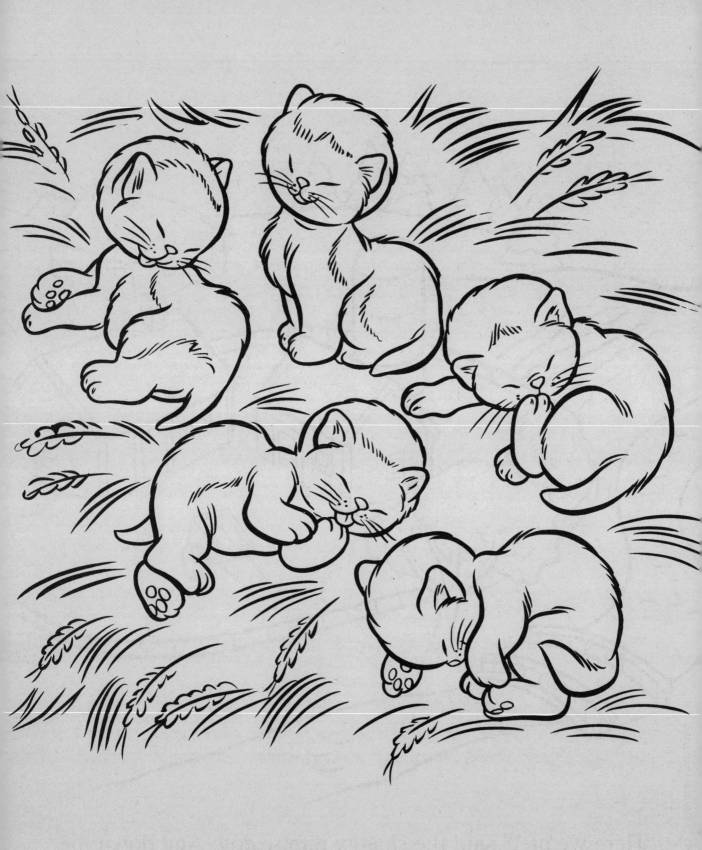

In the middle of the farmyard were the five
bold and frisky little kittens.

In a flash, the mother cat was beside her shy kitten, licking her all over with her warm red tongue. "Where have you been?" she cried. "We're all ready to start on a picnic."

And there for the picnic were the big gray hen, the duck, the goose, the rabbit, and the pig. The little gray mole and the big green frog were there, too!

They were all loaded down with baskets and boxes, and
all with arms full, they trudged off to the orchard.

The kittens scampered busily around, sampling everything.

They turned their noses up at the chickens' tasty beetles,
but they tried the carrots and the cabbage.

Yum, yum, yum! How good it all was! Everyone was just beginning to feel comfortable when suddenly the frog jumped straight into the air. "Help! Run!" he cried.

Everyone scrambled after him and tumbled into the water.
"What is it?" asked the shy little kitten. "A bee!" groaned
the frog. "I bit a bee!" One side of his mouth was puffed
up like a balloon. Everybody laughed. Even the frog.
They couldn't help it!

The shy little kitten stood off to one side. She felt so good that she turned a backward somersault, right there. "This is the best day ever," said the shy little kitten.

The Fuzzy Duckling

Early one morning, a small fuzzy duckling went for
a walk. He walked through the sunshine. He walked
through the shade.

In the long striped shadows that the cattails made,
the duckling met two frisky colts.

"Hello," said the duckling. "Will you come for
a walk with me?"

But the two frisky colts would not.

So on went the little duckling, on over the hill.

On the other side of the hill, the duckling found three
spotted calves, all resting in the shade.

"Hello," said the duckling. "Will you come for
a walk with me?"

But the sleepy calves did not want to walk.
So on went the duckling.

In the distance, the fuzzy duckling sees a goose and a turkey.

Help the fuzzy duckling get to them.

START

FINISH

Next, the duckling met four noisy turkeys . . .

. . . and five white geese . . .

. . . and six lively lambs with thick, soft fleece.

But no one would come for a walk with the fuzzy
duckling. So on he went, all by his lone.

Along the way, he met seven playful puppies . . .

. . . and eight hungry pigs. "Won't you come for a walk
with me?" asked the fuzzy duckling.

"You had better walk straight home," said the pigs.
"Don't you know it's suppertime?"

What are the pigs having for dinner?
Connect the dots to find out.

"Oh," said the duckling. "Thank you."
But which way was home?

Just as he began to feel quite unhappy, he heard a
sound in the rushes nearby. . . .

What do you think is making the noise?
Draw it.

The noise in the rushes is coming from the ducks!
"At last," said the mother duck. "Here is our lost
baby duckling."

"Get in line," called the other ducklings.
"We're going home for supper."

So the lost little duckling joined the line, and away went the ten little ducklings, home for supper.

"This is the best way to go for a walk," said the happy little, fuzzy little duck.

The End

Color and Count!
How many colts did the duckling meet?
Count and color them.

ANSWER: 2.

How many calves did the duckling meet?

ANSWER: 3.

How many lambs did the duckling meet?

ANSWER: 6.

How many ducklings?